Espresso Yourself

VOLUME 1
DEC. 1, 2017 – DEC. 28, 2018

WRITTEN BY BRENT METCALF & MICHAEL CALLAHAN

ILLUSTRATED BY BRENT METCALF

Espresso Yourself: A Caffeinated Comic for Anxious Times - Volume 1
By Brent Metcalf and Michael Callahan

Illustrated by Brent Metcalf

Book design by ReformationDesigns.com

ISBN:978-1700159625

Distributed by **Bipster.net**

"For behold! Darkness shall cover the earth!"
—Isaiah 60:2

LIKE THAT'S A BAD THING. ANYWAY, A YEAR AGO I STARTED WORK AT CUPPA AND THAT HEDGEHOG WALKED THROUGH THE DOOR

AND A GREAT CARTOON STRIP WAS BORN!

IF NOTHING ELSE, IT HAS TAUGHT THE WORLD THAT THE ONLY ACCEPTABLE COFFEE IS ESPRESSO IN PURE FORM.

"For on that day, all frou frou drinks shall pass away! And they will behold espresso!"
—Archimedes 2:1

I WOULD SAY "THANK YOU" FOR BUYING THIS BOOK

BUT YOU AND I BOTH KNOW YOU ANNOY ME.

FOR YOU DISTURB MY BLISS WITH YOUR SAD REQUESTS FOR DISGUSTING ICE COLD FRAPPAWHATSITS WITH EXTRA DING DONGS ON TOP.

OR YOU IRRITATE ME WITH YOUR HALF CAF VEGETARIAN MISTY CREAMER SAUCE, OR THE USUAL SPRAY INSULATION FOAM THAT NORMAL HUMANS CAN SUCK DOWN GIVING THEM AN RF 15.

But I digress...

IN THIS BOOK IS WISDOM. STUDY IT. LEARN ITS WAYS.

ENLIGHTENMENT IS HERE! DARKNESS IS HERE!

NO ONE COMES UNTO THE DARKNESS BUT BY ESPRESSO!

Here endeth the lesson.

NOW, GO AWAY.

3

BY BRENT METCALF & MICHAEL CALLAHAN

© 2018 BRENT METCALF & MICHAEL CALLAHAN

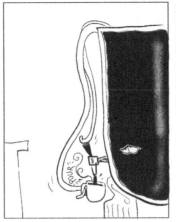
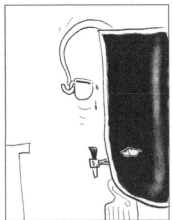

© 2018 BRENT METCALF & MICHAEL CALLAHAN

© 2018 BRENT METCALF & MICHAEL CALLAHAN

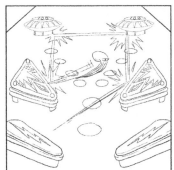

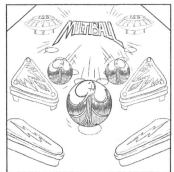

THE POP CULTURAL PARADIGM CAN SHIFT *ANY TIME NOW*

© BRENT METCALF & MICHAEL CALLAHAN

© 2018 BRENT METCALF & MICHAEL CALLAHAN

NICE SEEING YOU AGAIN, JANE.

SHE THINKS I'M A DOG WALKER, AND NOW EVERYONE AT THE OFFICE WILL THINK I'M A LOSER.

SHE'LL FORGET SHE EVEN SAW YOU. NOBODY CARES.

NO. NO. NO. NO. NO. NO. NO.

WHAT'S WRONG?

Posted 13 seconds ago

Since leaving us Zeph's career has gone to the dogs. "Woof!"

72 Likes

Posted 46 seconds ago

Since leaving us Zeph's career has gone to the dogs. "Woof!"

179 Likes

I CAN NEVER SHOW MY FACE AGAIN.

"WOOF"? THE GREATEST CULTURAL GENIUS SINCE KUBRICK AND SHE HAS ME SAYING "WOOF"?!

SHE AND I HAVE LIKE 50 KAJILLION FRIENDS IN COMMON.

I ONCE WROTE A FIFTY PAGE DISSERTATION ON PAUL THOMAS ANDERSON AND THE FILMIC QUEST TO PORTRAY AMERICAN HOSTILITY AND HUBRIS ON FILM!

WAIT... REALLY?

WELL... IN MY HEAD.

WHEN WORK WAS SLOW.

AND I WAS FLOATING IN THE ESPRESSO VAT.

BATHED IN THAT SWEET AMBROSIA.

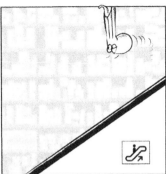
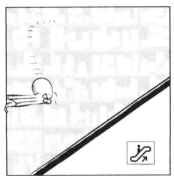

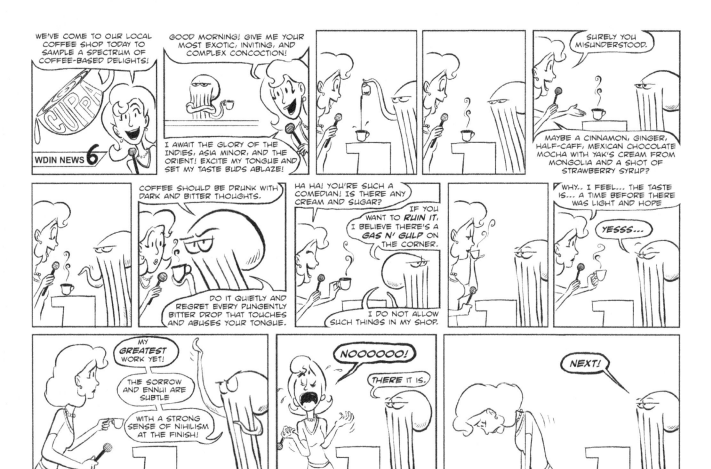

© 2018 BRENT METCALF & MICHAEL CALLAHAN

© 2018 BRENT METCALF & MICHAEL CALLAHAN

OL' GRUMPY: GERMANY
• WELL OFF
• BEER BELLY (WORKING ON IT)
• SECRET CRUSH ON ANGELA MERKEL (KIND OF LOOKS LIKE A BEAR)

ZEPH: ICELAND
• HIPSTER ZEITGEIST
• IMAGINES HIMSELF A DISRUPTOR
• THINKS CHOICE IMPROVES HIS IMAGE

RHINOMAN: ENGLAND
• DOESN'T THINK STRAIGHT
• MUMBLES AND BELCHES FREQUENTLY
• WATCHED FAWLTY TOWERS WAY TOO MANY TIMES

ARCHIMEDES: HATES SOCCER
• HATES SOCCER
• HATES SOCCER
• PLANNING TO HIDE IN A VAT OF ESPRESSO FOR THE MONTH

© 2018 BRENT METCALF & MICHAEL CALLAHAN

41

THE SIX STAGES OF PINBALL

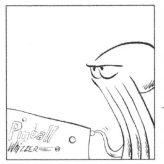

STAGE 1: THE THUMP AS THE QUARTERS GO IN

STAGE 2: A RAMP SHOT MADE

STAGE 3: EXTRA BALL

STAGE 4: MULTI BALL

STAGE 5: JACKPOT SHOT DURING MULTIBALL

STAGE 6: REPLAY!

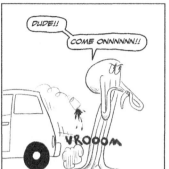

© 2018 BRENT METCALF & MICHAEL CALLAHAN

© 2018 BRENT METCALF & MICHAEL CALLAHAN

© 2018 BRENT METCALF & MICHAEL CALLAHAN

© 2018 BRENT METCALF & MICHAEL CALLAHAN

MEANWHILE, BACK IN THE LAB...

ZEPHYR RECOVERS FROM A DOSE OF ARABICA ARRHYTHMIA, THE WORLD'S MOST DANGEROUS COFFEE NOT APPROVED FOR VERTEBRATES.

THE STRANGE DREAMS ARE ENDING.

WHERE AM I...?

WHAT DAY IS IT...?

DAY 8, THE SUBJECT WAKES.

SCIENCE NEWS

© 2018 BRENT METCALF & MICHAEL CALLAHAN

SO, LET'S GET THIS STRAIGHT, YOU LIVE IN A BARN, PARTY ALL NIGHT...

YOU HATE HALLOWEEN, STAR WARS, AND DISNEY.

YOU LISTEN TO OPERA AND SING BARBERSHOP.

YOU ARE AN ELITIST SNOB WHO ONLY DRINKS ESPRESSO.

COULD YOU BE MORE WEIRD OR MORE OFFENSIVE TO MODERN GENTLE SENSIBILITIES OF TASTE AND GENERAL HIPNESS?

OF COURSE YOU COULD.

YOU PLAY VIOLA.

SIGH

© 2018 BRENT METCALF & MICHAEL CALLAHAN

SO WHAT DO FOLKS AROUND HERE DO FOR THANKSGIVING?

THEY EAT DEAD THINGS

ARE YOU VEGAN?

I WORK FOR BEARS.

MY ONLY FRIEND IS A HEDGEHOG.

I PARTY ALL NIGHT WITH GOTH CHICKENS...

I BELIEVE IN THE HARMONY OF ALL CONSCIOUS BEINGS WITHIN THE GREAT PANOPLY OF CREATION THROUGHOUT THE UNIVERSE.

HIS NAME WAS FRED.

HE LIKED SUMMER SUNRISES AND BEETHOVEN

HE HARMONIZES WELL WITH THE ZINFANDEL.

ARE YOU FEELING OK?

WHY DO I FIND POOP EMOJIS LESS THAN WHOLLY SATISFYING?

WHY AM I FINDING THE AROMA OF PUMPKIN SPICE LATTES INSUFFERABLE?

IS DISNEY JUST MINING OUR COLLECTIVE CHILDHOOD FOR PROFIT?

LOOK WHAT YOU'VE DONE TO HIM!

SUBJECT IS EXHIBITING A MORE ACUTE SENSITIVITY TO THE VAPID NATURE OF MODERN CULTURE.

THANKS FOR READING!

We started Espresso Yourself on a whim (and probably over a cup of espresso) almost two years ago. It's definitely a surreal experience to be publishing this collection of our first year's worth of comics.

If you're reading this right now, you have supported us in one way or another and we just wanted to take a moment to express our heartfelt gratitude to you for joining us on the creative journey of bringing Archimedes and the gang to life.

Thanks so much for your love and support.

If you enjoyed the antics of the Cuppa crew, make sure to stay in touch with us at www.espressoyourself.net

Brent and Michael
October, 2019

ABOUT THE CREATORS

Michael Callahan is a writer and musician who lives in Moline, IL. His writings have been published by Necropolis/Splore books, The Philadelphia Inquirer, and the River Cities Reader. Michael also is a four time winner of the Quad Cities Playwrights Festival and has had his works produced at New Ground Theater. Michael is a frequent performer locally with "It's a Mystery", Quad City Opera and Genesius Guild. Mr. Callahan also is the music director of Bethel Wesley United Methodist Church in Moline, and the Front Line director of Davenport's Chordbusters barbershop chorus.

Brent Metcalf is an artist and technologist. He graduated from Rock Island High School in 1989, the University of Illinois, Urbana-Champaign in 1995. He's been drawing since he could hold a crayon, and intended to become a professional comic book artist, but somehow got detoured into the IT field for a couple of decades. Now he's pursuing freelance illustration, cartooning, and video editing. His work has been published in The Absolute Essential Zombie Coloring Book, The Many Moods of Maggie Mu children's book, The ABC's of Conscious Capitalism children's book, and the Against the Odds YouTube series. Brent currently lives in the Pacific Northwest and is ever vigilant in his quest for the perfect latte. You can see his work at www.bipster.net.

Made in the USA
Monee, IL
04 November 2019